The Biggest Fish In The World

The Biggest Fish In The World

by A.W. Reed

A.H. & A.W. REED

WELLINGTON   SYDNEY   LONDON

First published 1974

A. H. & A. W. REED LTD
182 Wakefield Street, Wellington
51 Whiting Street, Artarmon, NSW 2064
11 Southampton Row, London WC1B 5HA
also
29 Dacre Street, Auckland
165 Cashel Street, Christchurch

ISBN: 0 589 00848 X

The stories in this book were, with one exception, first
published in the series *Traditional Tales of New Zealand*

*Typeset by New Zealand Consolidated
Press Ltd, Wellington.
Printed by Kyodo Shing Loong Ltd,
Singapore.*

CONTENTS

For Joanna and Richard
from
Grandad

THE BIGGEST FISH IN THE WORLD

LONG LONG AGO, say the Maoris of New Zealand, there were no islands in the ocean that lies at the bottom of the world.

One day a magic canoe came sailing across the sea. On board the canoe were five brothers. The one who was called Maui was a mischievous young man. He was the youngest of the five brothers. He had often made them angry because of the tricks he played on them.

"We'll stop here," Maui said. "This is a good place for fishing."

He threw his magic bone hook overboard and watched as it shimmered in the water at the end of the fishing line.

Soon he felt a tug on the line and shouted, "I've caught a fish."

The fish that Maui had caught was the biggest fish in the whole world. His brothers helped him pull it up. It was far bigger than you could ever imagine. It was so big that its tail was far away out of sight.

The big fish lay on the top of the water and tried to get rid of the hook. Maui's canoe was tossed about until at last it was thrown up on to the fish's back.

Maui jumped out of the canoe.

"Stay here," he said to his brothers. "I'm going to pray to the gods to bless this fish. It belongs to me. Don't you dare touch it while I'm away."

As soon as he was gone his brothers began to cut the flesh to pieces with their sharp knives.

When he came back Maui was angry.

"You have spoilt my fish!" he cried. "Couldn't you see that it is really an island? I wanted it to be nice and smooth. You have cut it up into hills and valleys."

It was a long time ago when Maui caught his big fish. It is now called the North Island of New Zealand. Perhaps it was a good thing that Maui's brothers cut the fish to pieces with their knives. The people who live on it now love the steep hills and valleys. They climb the mountains, they swim in the lakes, and fish in the mountain streams.

You see, the North Island of New Zealand is shaped just like a fish. Some of the Maori people who live in these islands say that the South Island is Maui's canoe and that the North Island is his fish – the biggest fish in the whole world!

In the stories in this book you will be able to read some more stories that are told about the wonderful fisherman, Maui, starting from the time when he was a tiny baby.

Sun, Sea And Star

illustrated by Roger Hart

THE BOY MAUI

A bunch of seaweed was being tossed about on the waves of the sea. Seagulls looked down at it, screaming and wailing as they fluttered round it. And no wonder, for a tiny baby was wrapped tightly in the seaweed. The baby's name was Maui—little Maui, the son of Taranga. Taranga had four sons. When little Maui came she thought he was dead, so she cut off her hair, wrapped the baby in it, and threw him into the sea.

But the gods of the sea were kind to the baby. They made a raft of seaweed and put Maui into it. Then the winds came and blew the seaweed raft away from the land.

Presently the raft was washed up on to a sandy beach. The sun was hot. The seaweed became dry and fell away. Baby Maui felt hot and thirsty. He began to cry. Old Tama, who lived in a house on top of the cliff heard him crying. He ran down to the beach and picked the baby up.

"There, there," he said, stroking his tiny head. "I know what's the matter with you. Poor little fellow. You're thirsty."

Tama carried the baby back up the path to his home and gave him something to drink. Then he put Maui into a flax bag and tied it to the roof. The baby was very comfortable there. He laughed

at Tama and waved his arms, and at last he fell
asleep.

"Well, this has been a funny day," old Tama
thought. "Here is a baby that has come out of the

sea. I wonder where his mother is. And what am I going to do with him now that he's here!"

It was a long time since Tama had children of his own, but he tried to remember how they had to be looked after. When the baby woke up, he took him out of the bag and gave him something to eat and drink. He put him in a sunny place and gave him some sticks to play with.

Maui was very happy in the old man's home. Soon he was able to walk and then to run about. Tama showed him how to go down the path to the beach, so that he could swim in the water.

As he grew older he learnt many things from the old man. He learned how to talk to the birds, and to play with the fishes. He played games with Tama, and listened to the stories he told as they sat by the fire at night. He began to grow tall and strong. He learned about the ways of birds and animals, and magic that helped him to make friends with them.

One day, when he was nearly grown up, he said to Tama, "Now I want to go back to my own people."

"Yes, you will have to go back to your own people," Tama said sadly. "You will leave the old man who has tried to teach you while you were growing up. You will do many wonderful things when you are older, Maui. Now go quickly my son. The world is waiting for you."

MAUI COMES HOME

Maui ran along the beach. He climbed up the hills and ran through the forests until at last he came to the place where his mother and father lived. He saw a large house and hurried towards it. Some young men were playing in front. They were throwing darts at the little wooden man on top of the house. A dart went *thump* against the house and one of the boards fell off.

Taranga rushed out to see what had happened. She saw the board lying on the ground and knew that one of her sons had knocked it off.

"Who did that?" she asked.

"Not me," said the oldest brother.

"Not me," said the next brother.

"Not me," said the next brother.

"Not me," said the next brother.

"If it wasn't one of you, then who was it?" asked Taranga.

"It was him," they all said together, pointing at Maui. They didn't know he was their brother and thought it would be a good idea if the stranger got into trouble.

"You were naughty to do this," Taranga said to him.

"I'm sorry," said Maui. "I'll put it back for you, if you'll let me stay with you."

"All right. You can stay here for a while. What's your name?"

"Maui."

"That's funny," said Taranga. "All my sons are called Maui too. Come inside, little Maui. I'll call you Maui Five."

After they had eaten their evening meal Taranga called her sons together.

"Something strange has happened," she said to them. "I have four sons—Maui One, Maui Two, Maui Three, and Maui Four. Now we have another Maui with us. I have called him Maui Five. Come here, Maui Five. Tell us who you are and where you come from."

"I am your son," said Maui Five.

There was a surprised look on Taranga's face.

"You can't be my son," she cried.

"Oh yes, I am. I came from the sea, wrapped in your hair."

His mother picked up a torch and looked hard at Maui. "What is my name?" she asked suddenly. ·

"You are my mother. Your name is Taranga. Tama told me your name."

She threw her arms round him and held him close.

"Yes, now I know you really are my son. When I wrapped you in my hair and threw you into the sea I thought you were dead. Now you have come back to me. You are indeed my son, and I love you.

You are Maui Five. Your name is Maui-tikitiki-a-Taranga—Maui wrapped in the hair of Taranga. You may live here with your brothers. I thought I had lost you, but now you will be my own little son again."

Maui had great fun with his brothers, but when he grew tired of them he used the magic he had learned from Tama to turn himself into a bird. Then he flew into the forest, so that he could talk to his friends the birds. When this happened his brothers were not very pleased with him.

There was only one thing that made him unhappy. He had never seen his father. Every night he went to sleep beside his mother. When he woke up in the morning her bed was empty, and he did not see her again until late in the afternoon.

"Where does our mother go after we go to bed?" he asked his brothers.

"We don't know and we don't care," they said.

"All right," Maui said. "I'll find out for myself."

The next night he stayed awake. When his mother was asleep he took some of her clothes and hid them. Presently, long before it was light, she got up and tried to find her clothes, but they were gone.

"Oh dear," she said, "I'll have to leave without them."

She wrapped an old cloak round her and tiptoed out of the door. Picking up an apron he had taken from her, Maui went outside to see what she was doing. He saw her bend over and lift up a big stone. There was a big hole under the stone. Taranga climbed into the hole—and then she was gone!

"That's funny," Maui thought.

He ran over to the hole and looked down. It was quite dark inside.

"Oh well, if she can go down there, I expect I can go down too."

He put the apron on. It was bright and shiny because it was made of pigeon's feathers. As soon as he put it on, he began to grow smaller, and the apron grew shinier and shinier. Presently he looked just like a beautiful pigeon. He spread his wings and flew down the hole. Down, down, down he went, down the dark hole until at last he came to another world, where a strange sun was shining.

Maui the pigeon perched on the branch of a tree and looked round to see if he could find his mother. Then he heard two people talking at the foot of the tree. One of them was Taranga. The other was a man Maui had never seen before. Maui guessed that this was his father.

He picked some berries with his beak and dropped them one by one on to his father's head.

"That's funny," the man said. "Some berries fell on my head just then. It must be time for the berries to fall."

Taranga laughed. "No. I saw a bird pick them up in his beak and drop them on you."

"Well, if it does it again, it had better look out for itself."

Maui picked a bunch of berries and dropped them on his father's head again. The man jumped up and threw a stone at the pigeon, but it hopped out of the way.

"Don't do that," Taranga said. "It's the most beautiful bird I've ever seen. Look how its feathers shine in the sun."

Maui's father took no notice. He kept on throwing stones at the bird. The pigeon hopped from side to side, but at last it fell off the branch and fluttered down to his feet.

Then it grew bigger and bigger—and there was Maui dressed in his mother's lovely apron.

"Oh!" cried Taranga, "this is your son, Maui Five. Not Maui One, or Maui Two, or Maui Three, or Maui Four, but Maui-tikitiki-a-Taranga, the little one I thought was dead. I wrapped him up in my hair and threw him into the sea, but now he has come back to us again. He has come by wind and wave, and now he really belongs to us."

So Maui Five lived happily with his mother and father—and all the pigeons in the bush were happy too, because he gave them the gay, shining apron that belonged to Taranga. If you ever see a pigeon in the New Zealand bush you will see that it still wears the beautiful apron that once belonged to Maui's mother.

MAUI ASKS HIS GRANDMOTHER
FOR FIRE

One day Maui was warming his hands in front of the fire.

"Where does fire come from?" he asked suddenly.

"We don't know," his brothers said. "Why do you always want to know things like that?"

"Well," said Maui Five, "what will happen if the fire goes out?"

"We won't let it go out," they said.

"The silly, empty-headed fellows!" Maui said to himself. "I'll put it out. Then perhaps they will want to know where it comes from."

And that's just what he did. When they woke up next morning the fire was dead.

Taranga came hurrying inside the house.

"The cooking fires are out," she cried. "What will we do?"

"I know," said a deep voice. An old man who lived in the village was speaking. "The only place we can get fire is from the under-world."

Taranga turned and looked at her sons. "That is where your grandmother lives," she said. "Who will get some more fire from her?"

"Not me," said Maui One. "It's too dark and dangerous down there."

"Not me, not me, not me," said Maui Two, Maui Three, and Maui Four.

"I'll go," said Maui Five.

"Oh, thank you," his mother said. "This is what you must do. When you get to the under-world you must be very careful. Go to your grand-mother's house. You can't mistake it, because you will see a bright fire burning inside. Go up to her and tell her that you are her grandson. Tell her that your mother has asked you for some fire because her fire has gone out. Then you must do exactly what she tells you."

"I'll look after myself," Maui said as he ran out of the door.

It was a long while before he reached the under-world. When he got there he soon found his grand-mother's house because a fire was burning brightly in the darkness.

"Hullo," he shouted. "Is anyone at home?"

"Who's there?" he heard an old woman say.

"It's me, Maui."

"I know lots of Mauis. What is your mother's name?"

"Taranga. I am her youngest son. They call me Maui Five."

The old woman laughed. "I've heard all about you, Maui Five. Come inside and make yourself comfortable."

Maui looked at his grand-mother. She was very tall and Maui felt just a little frightened.

"I've come to ask you for some fire. Ours have all gone out."

"That will be easy," the old woman said.

She pulled out one of her finger-nails. She put it on the end of a stick. As she gave it to Maui it burst into flame.

"Carry it carefully," she said. "I've only got ten finger-nails. When they've gone there will be no more fire anywhere in the world."

Maui thanked his grand-mother and started back home. He was not so frightened now, and he wanted to know how to make fire without carrying round anyone's finger-nails. He hid behind a tree and threw the burning finger-nail away. Then he went back and knocked on the door of his grand-mother's house.

"Please, Grandma," he said. "I've lost the fire you gave me."

"You naughty boy," she said crossly. "You must be more careful. Here is another. See you don't lose it this time."

Maui took it, but he threw it away again and went back for another and another, until she had used up nine finger-nails. When Maui asked for another, she was very cross indeed.

"Here is my last finger-nail," she shouted. "Never let me see you again."

She threw it at him. It fell on the ground and burst into flame. Maui was really frightened this time. The fire roared all round him. He ran away as fast as he could, but the fire kept up with him. The sheet of flame raced across the ground, burning up everything in its path. Maui could not run fast enough and was afraid of being burnt up. He said some magic words and changed himself into a hawk, and flew away—but the flames caught up with him and burnt his feathers. That is why the hawk's feathers are still brown.

He changed himself into a fish and dropped into a swamp with a big splash. But the fire was so hot that the water began to boil. It seemed as though the whole world would soon catch on fire. Then Maui remembered the gods that Tama had told him about when he was a young boy. He asked them to help, and they sent rain to put out the fire.

Then Maui's grand-mother hid the fire that was burning in her house. She hid it in the trees—the kaikomako, the mahoe, and the totara trees. The fire is still there, because men soon learned to rub the wood from these trees together to make fire whenever they needed it.

So in the end Maui gave something to his mother and his brothers and all the people in the world— the gift of fire that can be kindled whenever it is needed.

MAUI STOPS THE SUN

Maui was much older, but he still lived in the same village with his mother and his brothers. No one was really happy there, because the days were so short and the nights were so long. The sun raced across the sky so fast that there was no time for people to do what they wanted.

"Why don't you do something about it?" Taranga asked Maui.

"Oh no," his brothers cried. "Not Maui Five!"

Maui Five smiled. "It's all right," he said. "This time it's not my idea. Mother Taranga wants the sun to go more slowly, so we'll have time to do what we want while it's light—and if Taranga wants that, it's up to us to do it. Come on boys, let's get busy."

"What do we have to do?"

"First of all we'll get the women to make long flax ropes. They must be very strong. Then we'll carry them to the edge of the world. I'll show you how to get there."

That was how it all began. A few days later the five Maui brothers were hiding behind some big rocks waiting for the sun to come up. They had made a big snare with flax ropes and spread it across the sky to catch the sun when he began his journey across the sky.

It was very cold in the early morning air. The four older brothers stamped their feet and clapped their hands to keep warm.

"Be quiet," Maui Five whispered. "The sun will be up soon and then you'll be warm enough, I promise you. That is why you are to keep hidden behind these rocks. I don't want him to see you before I'm ready. When he comes out of the place where he sleeps at night he is so hot that you would be burnt to ashes if you were out in the open. Look! He's coming now."

Suddenly everything became light as the sun bounded up from his sleeping place.

"Pull the ropes! Pull the ropes quickly," shouted Maui Five. His brothers pulled, and the rope snare fell over the sun's head and shoulders.

"Let me go!" he shouted. "Let me go, you are hurting me."

"I'll hurt you more if you don't keep quiet," said Maui Five, banging him on the head with his magic fish hook.

"Help! Help! Let me go!"

" Not until you promise to go more slowly across the sky. We need longer days so we can do our work before it grows dark. Do you promise to go slow?"

"I promise," the sun sobbed. "I didn't know I was going too fast. Why didn't you tell me before?"

"Because I was the only one who knew where you came from," said Maui Five.

Bang! bang! went his fish hook again. "That's to make you remember," Maui said.

"There's no need to keep banging me on the head with your fish hook, Maui. I've promised to go slow, and I'll keep my promise."

"Fine," said Maui, giving him one last bang for good luck. "Come on, brothers. We'll go home now. We've plenty of time, because our friend the sun has promised to go slow."

So that was another of the many things that Maui did to help the people he lived with.

Tuna was the father of all the eels in the world. He lived in a swamp on the island called Te Ika a Maui. At the same time Maui was living with his wife, Hina, not far away from the swamp where Tuna had his home. Every day Hina went down to the swamp to fill her calabash with water.

One morning, while she was bending over to put her calabash in the water, she started back in alarm. She could see something long and black swimming in the water. It was Tuna, the father of eels. He lifted his head out of the water and said,

"Hullo, Hina. It's only me, Tuna. I expect you've heard about me."

"Yes," she said. "Maui has told me about you. He said I was never to speak to you."

"Well, you are speaking to me now, Hina. Come with me and I'll show you some of the treasures in my home under the water."

"No, I won't go with you. Maui said I was never to go with you."

"Oh, come on, Hina. I won't hurt you. It won't take long, and Maui will never know where you've been."

Hina didn't wait to hear any more. She turned round and ran home as fast as she could.

"What have you been doing all day?" Maui asked when he got home at night.

"Oh, nothing much," said Hina. "I brought water from the swamp and swept the floor and cooked a meal for you. That's all."

She didn't tell him what Tuna had said to her because she thought Maui might be angry.

When she went down to the swamp next morning she looked round carefully to see if Tuna was there, but she could not see him, so she scooped up some water with the calabash.

Suddenly the water was ruffled and Tuna came rushing up from his hole deep down under the swamp.

"There you are!" he said. "I knew you would come to see me this morning. Are you ready?"

"Go away," Hina said. "I don't want to have anything to do with you."

"Don't pretend you don't want to see my treasures," Tuna laughed.

He swung his tail round in a big circle and knocked her off her feet. She fell into the water. Tuna began to drag her towards his hole, but Hina managed to slip away before they got there. She swam to the bank with quick strokes, climbed out of the water, and ran home, sobbing as she went.

Maui was sitting in front of the house.

"What's the matter?" he asked when he noticed that she was crying.

"It's that Tuna," she said. "He knocked me into the water with his tail."

"Why?"

"He wanted me to look at the treasure he said he kept in his hole."

"And why didn't you look at it?"

"I was afraid."

"Why were you afraid?"

"I thought he might want me to stay with him for ever."

"Yes," said Maui slowly, stroking his chin. "Yes," he said again, jumping up. "He will be sorry by the time I've finished with him!"

"What are you going to do?" Hina asked.

"Never mind what I'm going to do. You just keep away from Tuna for the next few days."

Hina went inside the house while Maui went into the bush. He cut down young trees and made them into spades that would dig deep and fast. Taking a sharp knife in his hand he went down to the swamp.

Then he sat on the bank and watched the spades digging a long trench from the swamp right down to the sea. When it was finished he spread a net across the end of the trench.

Presently it began to rain. The little streams poured into the swamp and the water rose and filled the trench. It roared down to the sea carrying bushes and trees with it—and in the middle of the rushing water was Tuna, the father of eels. He was tossed from side to side until he was caught by the net Maui had spread at the end of the trench.

Maui lifted his knife and cut off Tuna's head with one clean stroke. It fell into the water and was swept out to sea. Then Maui cut off its tail and chopped it into little pieces.

But this was not the end of Tuna, father of eels. His head turned into a fish, his tail became the conger eel, and the little pieces all turned into the eels that swim in the rivers and streams of New Zealand.

That is why Tuna is known as the father of eels.

MAUI AND THE FIRST DOG

Maui went fishing with Ira, the brother-in-law of Hina. Ira caught so many fish that the bottom of the canoe was covered with them, but Maui did not catch one.

"You silly old man," Ira said to Maui. "Why don't you stay home and play with the children? That's all you are good for."

"You have been lucky this time," Maui said, "but we will not leave this place until I have caught a fish."

"Very well," said Ira. "Let down your line again."

Maui threw out his hook. Before long there came a tug on the line.

"I've got one," he shouted excitedly and began to pull it up. Ira pulled his line in at the same time —but when it came to the top both men could see that the fish was on Ira's line, not Maui's.

"I told you you couldn't catch fish," Ira said. "If it wasn't for me we wouldn't have any to take home."

Maui was so angry he was hardly able to speak. They paddled the canoe back to land. When they reached the beach Maui called to Ira to jump out and lift the outrigger. While he was bending over and lifting it on to his back, Maui threw down his paddle and jumped on to Ira's back. Ira fell and lay helpless, with the outrigger resting on him.

Maui stamped on him until Ira's back became long. Fur grew on him, his legs and arms became short, he grew a tail, and his head was like a dog's. Ira had changed into a dog, a furry Maori dog, the very first of all the dogs in the world.

When Maui walked up the beach he was met by Ira's wife.

"Where is Ira?" she asked.

"I left him by the canoe," he said with a laugh, but his eyes were not smiling. "Go and help him. If you can't find him, call him. Call 'Mo-i, mo-i,' and he will answer."

She hurried across the beach, but she could not see Ira anywhere. She called him, but there was no answer. Then she remembered what Maui had said. She cried, "Mo-i, mo-i, mo-i," and at once a strange animal ran from behind the canoe and jumped up at her.

Then Ira's wife knew what had happened. She turned round and went back to her home. Tears were running down her face, but the dog that was once her husband was quite happy being petted by the village children.

MAUI AND THE STARS

Maui was growing old. He was still full of fun, and his brothers still wondered what new ideas he would think up next. He had two sons. They were both grown up. One day he called them to come to him.

"My sons," he said, "everyone tells me bad stories about you, and they make me very sad. You are trouble makers, and no one wants you in the village any more."

He put his hands on their shoulders.

"Don't be sad," he said. "I can't let you stay here, so I'm going to send you away, but you will never be forgotten. I'm going to turn you into stars."

His sons laughed at their father. "That will be the day!" they said. "No one can turn men into stars, not even you, father."

Maui said nothing. He said some magic words and touched their faces with his fingers, and they became light as feathers. Then he lifted them in his hands and threw them up into the sky.

They never came down again. If we look at the night sky we can still see them twinkling up there. One of them is the morning star and the other is the evening star.

Taki, who was an old man, watched Maui throw his two sons into the sky. He was so old that he had become tired of living in this world.

"Make me into a star too, please, Maui," he said.

Maui looked him up and down.

"You are too fat," he said. "You are too heavy for me to throw you up into the sky."

"I *do* want to go up there with your sons," Taki said. "I *do* want to twinkle in the sky every night. Can't you help me?"

"I might," Maui said. "What will you give me?"

"I'll give you my best tiki."

"What else?"

"What about this beautiful greenstone mere?"

"Yes, that will do," Maui said. "Come with me."

He took Taki to the place where vine roots hang down from the sky.*

"I will help you to climb up them," said Maui. "Then you can sit up there in the sky and twinkle like a little star for ever."

So that was just what Taki did, and he is still sitting up there, twinkling away for ever. The Maoris call it Taki-ara—the guiding star. Taki was quite happy, and so was Maui, sitting by his fire, rubbing Taki's greenstone mere in his hands and looking at the greenstone tiki shining in the firelight.

* See **"Tawhaki's Long Climb"** in *Dreaming and Climbing* in this series.

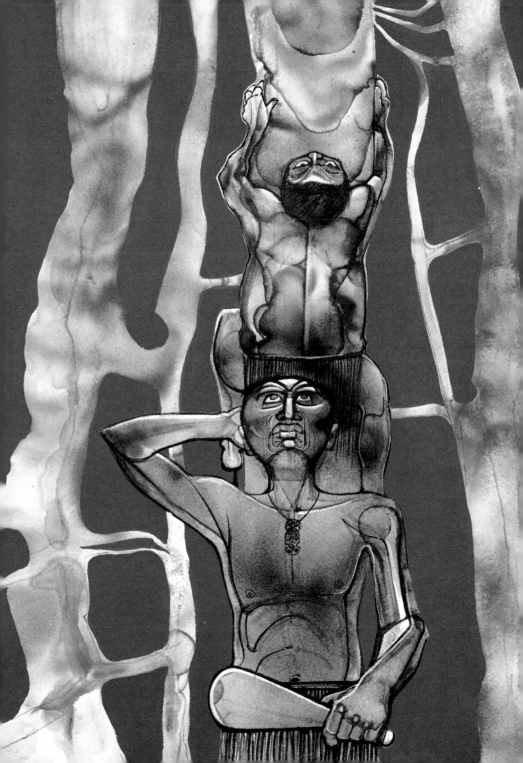

Bitterns And Bones

illustrated by Rob Taylor

RATA'S FATHER AND THE BAD BITTERN

While Rata was still a young boy, his father had gone away from home and had never come back. Rata's mother was very sad. She did not know what had become of her husband.

"When you grow up, you must go and look for him," she told Rata. "I expect he has been killed by someone. You must find out who he is and punish him."

"Yes, I will, Mother," Rata promised her.

When he was grown up, he remembered his promise.

"It is time to go now," he said to her. "I will take some of my friends with me, and we will find out what happened to my father. If anyone has killed him, I will punish him."

So one day he left home with six of his friends. They all had their weapons with them. After many days they came to the house of Matuku, who was a bad man. He was not at home, but an old woman was there. She was Matuku's slave.

"Who are you? What do you want?" the old woman asked, when she saw Rata and his friends.

"My name is Rata. I'm looking for my father."

"Rata," the old woman said wonderingly. "Rata! Where have I heard that name before? Let me think."

She sat down and put her head in her hands. Presently she looked up.

"I know. A man came here many years ago. Before he was killed he told me he had a little boy called Rata. Are you his son?"

"I expect so," Rata said. "You said this man was killed. What happened to him?"

"Oh, he came here and talked to Matuku, who lives here. I am his slave."

"What happened then?"

"Oh, Matuku never lets anyone stay here. He kills everyone. I'm the only one he lets alone. He keeps me here to work for him. When this man, who may well be your father, wasn't looking he killed him and ate him. Then he gave his bones to the sea fairies. They took them away. They keep them in their house far away across the sea."

"I'm sure this man was my father," Rata said. "I'm going to punish him for what he did. Will you help me?"

"Yes, I'll help you," she said. "I'm tired of working for Matuku. He is a bad man. I'll tell you what to do. First of all you must light a big fire in front of the house. Matuku will hurry home to find out what is happening. You must hang a noose of rope over the door. As soon as he goes in, drop it over his shoulders and pull it tight."

Rata thanked the old woman. Soon they had a

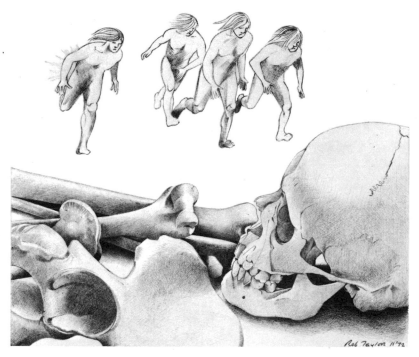

fire lit and a rope noose hanging over the door.
Then they hid behind the house with one end of
the rope in their hands. Rata was lying on the roof
so he could drop the noose over Matuku's shoulders.

When Matuku saw the smoke he ran home as fast
as he could. He stopped at the door and called to
the old woman.

"What is happening?" he asked. "Something
strange is going on here."

"Yes," she said. "Some men came here this
morning. They are inside the house. Go and see
what they are doing."

Matuku drew his weapon. Holding it in his hand, he rushed through the door—but at that moment Rata dropped the noose over his head and shoulders.

"Pull!" he shouted, and his friends pulled the rope as tight as they could.

Rata jumped down from the roof.

"I am Rata," he said. "You killed my father. Now I'm going to punish you."

Matuku laughed in his face. "Do you think you can kill me, little man?" he asked. "You'll be sorry you said that. I'm stronger than you."

Rata drew his weapon and cut off one of Matuku's arms; and then the other. Matuku laughed louder still. Rata's friends let the rope go and rushed round to the front of the house to see what had happened.

What a surprise they got! Matuku's legs grew thin, his hair turned into feathers, he grew smaller and smaller, and slipped out of the noose. He had changed into a bittern, a bird with a big voice that lives in the swamps.

They tried to catch him, but he ran too fast and was soon lost in the rushes of the swamp. They could still hear his voice. Matuku the bad bittern was still laughing at them.

So Rata went home with his friends, and told his mother what had happened to Matuku, the man who had killed his father.

"That is good," she said. "Now all you have to do is to find your father's bones, and bring them home."

RATA AND THE CANOE

The bones of Rata's father were hidden in the house of the sea fairies on an island. Rata wanted to punish them, but he had no canoe.

"I know what I'll do," he said. "I'll go into the forest and cut down a big tree. I'll make it into a canoe. When it is finished my friends will come with me. We'll kill the men who took my father away, and we'll bring back his bones and put them in his own home."

He went into the forest to find a tall straight tree. When he found one that pleased him he cut it down with his stone adze. Rata cut off the branches and went home for his tea.

While he was asleep that night, strange things were happening in the forest. All the birds and the insects, who are the children of Tane, the forest god, came together and looked at the fallen tree.

"Dear, dear!" they said. "Tane won't like this! That silly boy Rata cut down the tree without asking if he minded. We'll have to put it back before Tane sees it."

They worked hard all night long trying to drag the tree back into place. It was really hard work. While the birds were holding it up the insects picked up all the tiny pieces of wood and bark and put them back in place. This is the song they sang as they worked.

Come together, bits of wood,
Bits of bark.
Hold together, bits of wood,
Bits of bark.
Hold together tight.
Stand up straight and tall
As you were before your fall,
Tall tree of Tane.

Next morning Rata went into the forest again to begin to make his canoe. When he got there he rubbed his eyes to make sure he was awake. To his astonishment the tree was standing up, straight and tall, just as if he had never cut it down. Then he thought that perhaps he had made a mistake and come to the wrong place—but no, he was sure this was the tree he had cut down.

"Oh well," he said to himself, "never mind. I'll have to begin all over again."

This time he worked more quickly. The tree soon came crashing down. Rata cut off all the branches. With his sharp adze he took off long curling shavings. When the sun was sinking behind the tree tops, a beautiful canoe lay on the ground.

"I'll finish it off tomorrow," he said, and went home to get his tea.

But when he went back next morning, there was no canoe to be seen. All through the night the tiny children of Tane had been working and working to put the tree back in its right place.

"Poor Rata will get into such trouble from Tane if he sees his beautiful tree cut down," they told each other.

Next day Rata went back early in the morning and cut the tree down again. Then he turned round, put his adze over his shoulder, and went home again. The birds were watching him from the tree tops. The insects were peeping out of their homes under the leaves, in the ground, and in cracks in the bark.

"Why do you think he went home?" they whispered to each other. "Perhaps he is tired. Well, come on. Let's get to work."

But Rata hadn't really gone away. He was hidden in the long grass, waiting to see what would happen to his canoe. He saw the birds flying down from the tree tops. He saw the insects creeping out of their holes. He saw the birds hold the tree in their beaks and pull it off the ground. He saw the insects carrying the tiny bits of bark and wood and putting them back on the tree. He heard the whirring of the birds' wings—and then the song they were singing:

> Come together, bits of wood,
> Bits of bark.
> Hold together, bits of wood,
> Bits of bark.
> Hold together tight.
> Stand up straight and tall
> As you were before your fall,
> Tall tree of Tane.

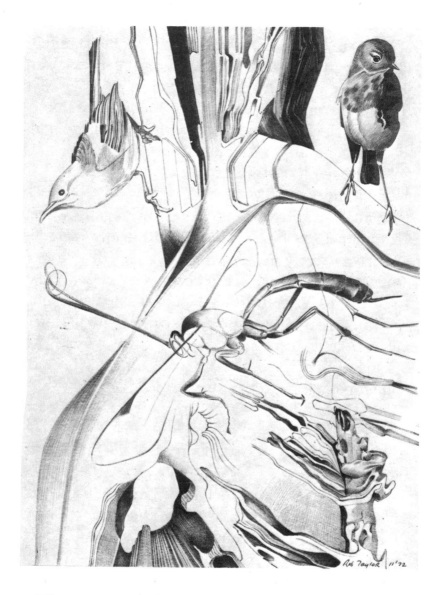

The song ended—and there was the tree, standing straight and tall waving its leaves in the wind.

Rata jumped up and rushed over to the birds and insects.

"Why are you doing this to me?" he shouted. "That was my canoe. You have no right to touch it. It belongs to me. Why did you spoil it?"

The birds and the insects crowded round him.

"You've been very naughty, Rata," they said. "It was wrong of you to cut down that tree."

"Why?" he asked in surprise. "Why shouldn't I cut down any tree I want?"

"Because every tree in the forest belongs to Tane. If you had asked him first he would gladly have let you cut any tree you wanted."

Rata hung his head. "I'm sorry," he said. "What do you think I should do? I only wanted a strong canoe to take me to the island where my father's bones are kept, so that I can bring them home."

"Tane will be glad to help you," the birds said. "You must tell him you are sorry."

"Oh Tane," Rata said. "I'm sorry I cut down your tree. Please forgive me."

A soft warm wind suddenly set all the leaves dancing on the trees.

"Tane forgives you," the birds sang. "Tane will help you! He has sent the warm wind to tell you he cares for you. Go home now and we will make a canoe for you."

So Rata went home. When he came back next morning a big beautiful canoe was waiting for him in the forest. The birds and insects had made it for him while he was asleep.

HOW RATA BROUGHT BACK HIS FATHER'S BONES

"How am I going to take the canoe through the forest and down to the sea?" Rata asked the birds and the insects.

"You must get your friends to help you," they said, "and we will gladly help too."

Rata went back to the village.

"Who will help me drag my canoe down to the beach?" he asked.

"We will. We will," they all said, and soon the big canoe began to slide through the forest. The men sang as they pushed and pulled with all their might. The birds took the ropes that Rata had tied on to the canoe in their beaks. They fluttered their wings and helped to pull it along the ground. Even the tiny insects pushed and pulled, until at last the canoe was dragged out of the forest and down the beach.

It went into the water with a big splash and rode proudly on the waves.

"Thank you, thank you," Rata cried. "Thank you, birds, thank you insects, thank you, Tane, and thank you, all my friends. Now, who will come with me in my canoe and help me to fight my enemies and bring back my father's bones so they can lie in peace in his own home?"

"We will come with you, Rata," all his friends

said. They brought their weapons from the village and put them carefully in the canoe.

"All aboard," shouted Rata, and everyone jumped into the canoe and paddled out to sea.

When the wind began to blow, Rata put up the sail, and the canoe picked up speed. Before long they reached the island where his enemies lived. They were wicked sea fairies who had killed his father. Afterwards they had taken away the bones of Rata's father and hidden them in their house.

"Quiet," whispered Rata as the canoe grounded on the sandy beach. They crept up the beach and hid among the flax bushes. The sun set and it grew dark. As the men watched they saw the fairies coming out of the sea and going into their house. Presently they saw lights in the house, and heard the fairies singing their magic songs. Two of the fairies were knocking the bones together, and the others were singing in time to the sound of the bones.

"Come on!" Rata whispered to his men who were standing ready with their weapons. They rushed through the door and surprised the bad fairies. Before long they were all dead. Rata picked up the bones of his father and wrapped them carefully in a new cloth.

"Tomorrow morning we will go home," Rata said, as they sat round the fairy fires. "They will never hurt or kill anyone again. No one will be afraid to come to this island again. But we shall not stay here any longer."

In the morning they carried the bones down to the beach and put them carefully in the canoe. Then they sailed back home and put the bones in a corner of the house.

But alas, no one knew that there were other bad sea fairies who had seen what they had done. While Rata and his men were paddling the canoe home, the bad fairies were swimming under water as quickly as they could. By the time Rata had put his father's bones away, the fairies had reached the land. They waited until it was dark, and then rushed towards the village.

Inside his house Rata heard a strange sound. It was his father's bones knocking together.

"Is that you, father?" he asked, and heard a soft voice whispering.

"I am the bones of your father," the voice said. "Hurry, Rata. My enemies will kill you if you don't call your friends. The sea fairies are nearly here."

Rata ran out of the house. He saw the fairies coming through the trees.

"Come to me!" he shouted. "The fairies are here!"

He was nearly too late. As the men from the village came running out the fairies rushed at them with their weapons and killed many of them.

"What shall I do?" Rata thought, and seemed to hear his father's voice again.

"Sing the magic song you heard in their house on the island," it said.

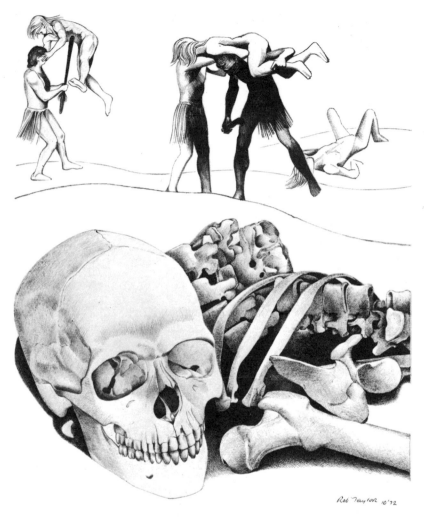

"I remember," said Rata. As soon as he began to sing the magic song, the sea fairies fell back and dropped their weapons. They turned round and ran away. Rata's friends chased them, killing many of them as they ran, until not one of the wicked sea fairies was left.

HATUPATU AND THE BIRD WOMAN

Hatupatu and his brothers were camping in the bush near Rotorua. They had built a tiny hut with branches of trees. Hatupatu was the youngest brother, so he had to stay behind while his brothers went out to hunt for birds. When they came back to the hut at night with the birds they had caught, they expected Hatupatu to have a cooked dinner ready for them. By the end of the day the boy was very tired because he had to spend a long time pulling feathers off the birds his brothers had caught, cleaning them, and putting them in calabashes filled with fat. When this work was finished, he had no time to rest. He had to hurry to get the dinner cooked.

His brothers were hungry when they got to the hut—and so was Hatupatu. But they would not let him have anything to eat until they had finished. Then there was nothing left but a few bones and a few bits of meat and vegetables. Poor Hatupatu was always tired and hungry.

One day he waited until his brothers had left on a hunting trip. Then he went into the hut and looked at the rows and rows of calabashes full of lovely, fat, tender birds.

"I'm going to have a good feed," he said to himself. "I don't care what they do to me."

He broke one of the calabashes. Then he sat

down, picked up one of the birds and ate it all up. When he had finished he ate another, and then another, until he was so full that he couldn't eat any more.

So he went and lay down in the long grass and was soon asleep. He woke up with a start. The sun was low in the sky and it was getting late.

"Oh dear, my brothers will soon be home," he thought. "What will they do to me when they find that I've forgotten to cook dinner for them and eaten some of their birds?"

He was frightened. "I know what I'll do," he said. "I'll cut myself with a knife so that the blood flows down, and perhaps they will think that I've been hurt by one of our enemies."

Soon his brothers came back. They went into the hut.

"Where are you, Hatupatu?" they called. "Where's our dinner?"

Hatupatu crawled out of the grass.

"I'm nearly dead," he said. "It's a wonder I'm not really dead. While you were away some of our enemies came here. They tried to burn down our hut, but I wouldn't let them, so they hurt me. But I drove them off. That's why I haven't been able to get dinner ready for you this afternoon."

"All right," his brothers said. "We'll let you off this time."

Hatupatu was very pleased. He lay down in the corner and laughed to himself. "I'll do it again tomorrow," he whispered.

But his brothers weren't really taken in by what he had said. They knew he was pretending. As soon as they left next morning, they hid behind the trees. They saw Hatupatu go into the hut. They saw him go to one of the calabashes and take out one of the birds. They saw him holding it in his hands and tearing large pieces out of it with his teeth.

They rushed into the hut with their weapons and kicked and beat him until he was black and blue all over. When he was nearly dead they tossed him out of the door and shouted, "Go away! We never want to see you again."

Poor Hatupatu lay on the ground for a long time without moving. The blood ran down his face, and his arms and legs and he was sore all over. He heard his brothers going away and then all was quiet. He helped himself up by holding on to the branch of a tree and walked slowly away. He didn't care where he went as long as it was somewhere away from his wicked brothers.

Presently he heard a strange sound in the bush. He stood very still and peeped through the leaves. His eyes grew quite round in surprise. There was a funny old lady with big wings and a long, sharp nose. It was more like a beak than a nose. She was watching a bird. Suddenly she darted forward and caught the bird with her long sharp nose.

"It really is a beak!" Hatupatu said. The bird woman heard him. She turned round and rushed towards him.

Hatupatu ran away as fast as he could. He heard the bird woman coming after him. The faster he ran the closer she seemed to be. He looked back and saw that she was flying in and out of the trees much faster than he could run. He tripped over a root and fell down.

"Got you!" laughed the bird woman.

She caught hold of the boy and tried to lift him. She flapped her wings but she couldn't get him off the ground. So she pulled him along behind her. Poor Hatupatu was bumped and banged until he was even more sore than he was before.

Presently they came to a very old house.

"This is where I live," the bird woman said. "In you go."

She gave him a push and he fell on the floor. Hatupatu was so tired that he fell asleep at once. When he woke next morning he heard a lot of birds singing.

"I wonder where they are," he thought. "They must be close."

He opened his eyes and looked up. Can you think where they were? They were right inside the bird woman's house.

"They are my pets," she said. "I keep them here in my house. When I am hungry I kill one of them and eat it."

She held out her hand and showed him a dead bird. "Eat this," she said.

"I can't," Hatupatu said. "It would make me sick."

"Don't be silly," the bird woman said. "Why don't you want to eat it?"

"It has to be cooked first."

"Well, I won't cook it. If you won't eat it like this, you'll just have to go hungry."

She ate it up herself, feathers and bones and all.

"You stay here," she said. "I'm going hunting now. If you try to run away my pet birds will see you. Then they will fly to me as quickly as they can and tell me where you are. You won't be able to hide from me. I'll find you where ever you are, and I'll eat you all up, just like a bird."

As soon as she had gone Hatupatu looked through the house to see what he could find, but there was nothing that he wanted. He went out of the door and began to run along a path through the bush. As soon as he had gone two of the pet birds fluttered out of the house and flew straight to the bird woman.

"Hatupatu has run away," they squeaked. "Come with us and we'll show you where he has gone."

Presently Hatupatu heard the flapping of big wings. He ran faster, but the sound came closer and closer. In front of him there was a big rock.

"Open up, open up!" Hatupatu shouted.

There was a creaking sound and the rock opened. Hatupatu jumped inside and the rock closed behind him. The bird woman banged on the rock.

"I know you are in there," she shouted. "Come out at once."

"No," said Hatupatu. "I'm staying here until you go away."

"Oh Hatupatu," the bird woman said softly. "I won't hurt you. I want to be your friend. Come out and I'll give you anything you want."

Hatupatu laughed. "Go away," he said again. "If I came out you would kill me."

"Very well," the bird woman said. "I'll go away now, but some day I'll catch you and then you'll be sorry."

The frightened boy waited for a long long time.

"Open up, rock," he said softly.

The rock opened and he poked out his head and listened. The only sound he could hear was the wind in the trees and the birds singing.

He jumped out and ran towards his home.

And then—oh dear—he heard the sound of the bird woman's wings. She had been hiding in the trees all the time.

Hatupatu ran as he had never run before—up the hill and down the other side, until at last he came to Rotorua where mud bubbles in the boiling pools and geysers throw up steam and boiling water.

Hatupatu ran across without stepping in them but the bird woman was not so lucky. As she jumped from one safe place to another she tripped and fell right into a pool of boiling mud—and that was the end of the bird woman!

Hatupatu went on until he came to Lake Rotorua. He jumped into the water and swam across the lake until he came to the island where his mother and father were living. It was getting dark, so he sat down beside a warm pool on this island and waited.

When it was quite dark he heard footsteps. Some-one was coming to the pool to fill a calabash with water. He put out his hand and caught hold of a leg.

"Who are you?" he asked.

" I am the slave of the old man and woman who live in the house nearest the pool," a woman's voice said.

"What are you doing here?"

"I've come to get water for them. They are thirsty. But who are you?"

"You'll find out soon enough," Hatupatu said. "Take me to your house."

The slave woman did as he asked. As soon as he was inside the house the old people saw him and cried, "It is our son Hatupatu!"

"Be quiet" Hatupatu whispered. "Where are my brothers? Please don't let them know I'm here."

"They are still out hunting," the old man said. "We expect them back tomorrow. Why have you come here without them?"

"They wouldn't let me eat any of the birds they caught, father. One day when they were out I was so hungry that I ate some. They came home at night and were very cross with me. They beat me until I was nearly dead, and tossed me out of the hut we had built. When they had gone away I got up and ran away too.

"Then I was chased by the bird woman who lives in the bush. She caught me and took me to her house, but I managed to get out and I started to run home to you. The bird woman chased me again but this time she wasn't able to catch me. I ran safely past the boiling pools, but she fell in. So I've come to you. Will you look after me?"

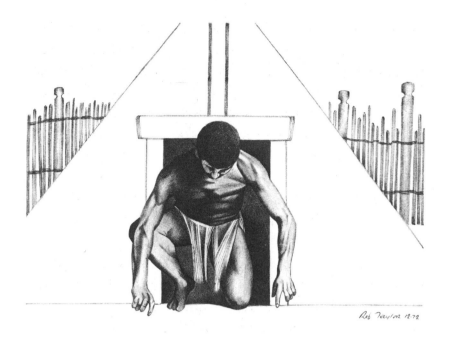

"Of course we will," said his mother. "We won't let your brothers hurt you. We'll hide you in the kumara pit. They will never find you there."

Early the next morning Hatupatu crept into the pit. It was very dark inside. He felt round with his hands and found a big stick. Then he lay down and waited for his brothers to come home.

Presently he heard them come home. Then he heard his father say to them, "Where is Hatupatu?"

"We don't know," they said. "He ran away while we were out hunting. When we got back he wasn't there. We looked for him for a long time. We think he must be dead."

"Oh no he isn't!" shouted Hatupatu.

He jumped out of the kumara pit. He lifted his stick over his head. It whirred round and round and then, bang! it hit the oldest brother on the head. Bang again, and the next brother fell down. The last of his three brothers was ready for him. His bird spear was in his hands. He threw it at Hatupatu, but the boy jumped aside and the spear went right into the kumara pit.

Hatupatu swung his stick round his head, and bang! it hit the last of the three brothers on the head.

"Oh dear," said his mother as she came out of her house and saw three of her sons on the ground. "Oh dear! You have killed them, Hatupatu! They are all dead. What shall I do?"

"They are not dead, mother," Hatupatu laughed. "They will wake up soon, and then they will have very sore heads. I don't think they will ever hurt me again."

*   *   *

When Hatupatu was grown up he was a great and strong soldier. No one ever beat him in a fight—and in Rotorua they still tell stories of Hatupatu and the wonderful things he did when he became a man.

But no one ever talks about his brothers who wouldn't feed him and tried to kill him while he was still a boy.

Dreaming And Climbing

illustrated by Trevor Plaisted

Tura had promised his friend Whiro that he would go with him in his canoe. When it was time to go he didn't want to leave his wife and baby son, but he felt that he must keep his promise.

"I will come back as soon as I can," he said to his wife.

Whiro was waiting for him.

"Come on," he shouted.

They set the sail, and soon they were out on the open sea. Presently Tura looked back. They had gone a long way from home. He couldn't see the land any longer. They sailed on all day and all night. When the sun came up the next morning they saw another land far away in front of them.

"Do you know what place that is?" Tura asked.

"No," said Whiro. "I've never seen it before. Let's go and see what it is like."

They sailed close to the beach. The wind was so strong and the canoe flew along so quickly that Tura was frightened.

"Please stop!" he called to Whiro. "The canoe is going too fast. Pull down the sail, or we'll crash into the rocks and be drowned."

Whiro pulled down the sail, but the canoe was caught in a strong current. It raced on as fast as before. It was swept under the branch of a tree. Tura jumped up. He caught hold of the branch and

swung himself into the tree. The canoe rushed on and on and was never seen again.

Tura climbed down the tree.

"What can I do now?" he thought. "I'm a long way from home. The canoe has gone and there's no way of getting back. Perhaps I'll never see my wife and my baby son Ira again."

He was very sad.

"Oh well, I might as well try to find out if anyone lives here," he thought.

He walked on for the rest of the day, but met no one. He lay down under a tree and went to sleep. Next day he kept on walking. His feet were sore and he was tired and hungry and thirsty. At last he came to an old house. It was falling to pieces, but an old woman was sitting by the door.

"Come inside," she said.

Tura went in. It was very dark inside the house, but the old woman was kind to him. She brought him something to eat, and gave him water to drink.

"Now you can lie down and tell me where you come from," she said.

"My friend and I came from another country," he told her. "We came here in a canoe, but it was swept away by the current and now I am all alone."

"Then you must come with me to our village tomorrow morning. Then you can meet my people. They will look after you."

When Tura came to the village the next morning

and saw the people who lived there he was very surprised. They were not like anyone he had met before. They lived in the branches of the trees and had tiny little heads and long arms and legs. They were friendly and asked him to stay with them.

"You must choose one of our young women for your wife," they said. Tura asked the most beautiful one he could see to be his wife. When she said yes he called her Tura-kihau. After that everyone called her Kihau.

Tura's wife brought him some meat and vegetables to eat, but the meat was raw and the vegetables were not cooked.

"Why didn't you cook the meat and vegetables?" Tura asked her.

Kihau looked at him in surprise.

"What is 'cooking'?" she asked.

"Surely you know what cooking is. You light a fire to cook anything you are going to eat. It makes everything tender and easy to eat."

"What is 'fire'?" Kihau asked.

"Oh dear, don't you even know what fire is? Look, I'll show you."

He found a flat board and told his wife to put her foot on it and hold it steady. Then he rubbed a pointed stick quickly along the board for a long time until at last smoke came from it. He dropped some dry grass on to the board, and soon it caught fire.

"There you are," he said when the grass began to burn. "That is what fire is."

He put dry flax and sticks on top, and soon the fire was burning brightly.

"Fire is very useful," Tura told all the people who had come to see what was happening. "It keeps you warm on cold nights, as well as being useful for cooking."

He showed them how to cook their food. When they had eaten it they were so pleased that they asked Tura to show them how to build houses, so they could live on the ground, and sleep by the fire at night, and cook their food every day.

Some time later Tura and Kihau had a baby boy and were very happy. One day, when the baby had grown into a big boy, Tura was resting in front of his house. His wife was sitting beside him.

"Tura," she said suddenly, "why have you got so many white hairs on your head?"

He laughed. "That shows that I'm getting old," he said, "but I have a long time to live yet."

"I don't understand," Kihau said. "Why shouldn't you go on living for ever?"

"When the men in my world get very old, they die, Kihau. Surely your people die when they are old?"

"No, Tura. We keep on living for ever."

She began to cry, and ran into the house. Tura thought very hard. Now he knew that his wife was really a kind of fairy, and that all her people were fairies too. He looked at his son and wondered if he would grow into a fairy too.

He went into the house to find his wife.

"I'm sorry," he said, "but I can't stay with you any longer. I must go back to my own country to live with the men and women of my own world. You see, Kihau, some day I must die and then you would be very unhappy. It is best for me to go now. I have a wife and a son in my own land, and I must see them again before I die."

A few days later he said goodbye to his fairy wife and son. He walked through the forest for two days until he came to the sea. He hoped that he would be able to see a canoe belonging to his own people, but there was nothing but empty sea and sky, so he built a tiny house to live in, and two platforms on which to keep food. One was tall enough to keep the food away from rats and ground birds. The other was close to the ground so that he would be able to reach the food easily when he was old and helpless; but he hoped that his people would find him and take him home long before that time came.

"Now to find food," he said, and walked along the beach. Presently he came to a place where a dead whale had been washed up on to the sand. He cut it up and put some of the flesh on the tall platform and some on the low platform to dry.

Many years passed by. Day after day he looked out over the sea, but no canoe ever came in to the land of the fairies. His hair was white all over; and it was hard for him to move about. He was thin and dirty and his hair was long. He lay on his bed remembering the time when he was young and happy with his baby son in his own country.

"Oh Ira!" he cried, thinking of him as he was when he had last seen him as a baby.

But of course Ira was now a man with children of his own. That night Ira had a dream. When he woke up he said to his wife, "I dreamed that I saw my father Tura last night. He left us a long time ago while I was still a baby. In my dream he seemed to be an old, old man, and he could not look after himself. What shall I do?"

His wife said. "It was only a dream, Ira. Your father must have died many years ago."

That night the dream came again. His father seemed to be calling him. "Oh Ira!" he cried, "Come and help me."

In the morning Ira went to his mother and told her about his dream.

"My father needs me," he said. "What shall I do?"

"You must go to him, of course," said his mother. "I will give you some of the food he likes best. I am very old now, my son, and your father is old too. Take the food with you and give it to him with my love. Tell him I am longing to see him again."

Ira asked his friends to help him. They pushed a big canoe into the water and paddled across the sea until they came to another country where a strong current began to carry the canoe towards the rocks at the end of a beach. They saw a house and two platforms close to a forest.

"This must be the place," Ira shouted, and strong arms paddled the canoe to the beach.

Ira was the first to go into the tiny house. He saw an old man lying there. He was very thin, and his white hair was long and dirty. The old man opened his eyes, but he could not move. He was trying to say something. Ira bent down to listen, and heard him say, "Oh Ira! help me."

"I'm here, father," he said softly. "You will be all right now. Look, mother has sent some of your favourite food. She wants you to come home."

Tura's eyes were shiny with tears as Ira lifted him tenderly in his arms and carried him down to the canoe. He made him comfortable and set out for home again. Tura lay on his back in the bottom of

the canoe. He looked up at the stars. He listened to
the song of the paddlers, and watched his grown-up
son. He was happy because at long last he was going
home.

THE ADVENTURE OF KAHUKURA

Kahukura was a chief. He was not like other men.

"Kahukura is young," one of the old men of the tribe said to his friends. "When the other young men are in the bush catching birds, he goes down to the edge of the beach and looks out across the water. Do you think he expects something strange to come out of the sea—something that will eat us all up?"

The old men looked over the fence and saw the young chief on the sandy beach. As they watched he turned and began to climb up the path towards them.

"Why don't you ask him what he is doing down there?" one of them asked.

"Not me!" said the old man. "Let him tell us himself when he's ready."

Kahukura said nothing to the people of his tribe, but he was excited. Night after night he had dreamed that he was walking on and on towards the end of the land. Every night he came closer. If his dream came once more he would reach the end and then he would find out what was waiting for him there. He was sure it would be something good.

And that night the dream did come. Kahukura seemed to be peeping through the bushes. There were sandy hills on each side of him and below them there was a beach. He heard the sound of music, and lights were dancing on the water. The music grew louder and the lights came closer. Kahukura wondered what would happen next. He was on the edge of a sandy cliff. Suddenly the sand gave way. He rolled down the cliff and gave a shout—and then he woke up—before he had time to find out where the dancing lights had come from and what they were doing.

"Perhaps the dream will go on tomorrow night," he thought, "and then I shall know why I have all these dreams. Perhaps I shall learn something that will help me to help my people. There are so many of them, and they are often hungry. Today the men didn't get any birds, and the fishers have to work all night to get enough fish for breakfast because they can only catch them one at a time. I wish I could do something to help. If the dream comes again, perhaps I'll learn something that will really help the tribe. Then they will look up to me."

But next night no dream came to Kahukura, or the next, or the next.

"I know the dream has something to do with the sea," Kahukura said to himself. "If the dream won't come to me, then I must try to find the place where the lights dance on the water at night and see what is there."

As soon as the sun came up he told his people that he was going away.

"I may be away for a long time," he said, "but I

shall come back. I may have some good news for you then, so watch out for me."

He went through the gate in the fence, down the path, and along the beach until he was lost to sight.

"I hope he knows what he is doing," said the same old man. "He is a strange young man, not like his father at all. But sometimes I think that in the end he will do more for his tribe than any of the chiefs we have ever had."

Kahukura knew where he was going. He knew the way because he had seen it all in his dreams. Sometimes he walked under a hot sun and sometimes he was wet through by the rain. Sometimes he had to scramble up hills, sometimes he had to cross deep rivers, and sometimes he had to swim to get round cliffs that came right down to the sea. At night he slept under the trees, wrapped tightly in his clothes to keep warm.

It took a long time to get to the beach where he had seen the dancing lights but one morning he reached the place he had seen in his dream. He hid in the bushes and waited until it was dark.

"At last I shall know what I have been waiting for all these weeks," he thought. He slid carefully down one of the sand hills and took cover behind a large rock.

He waited for a long time but nothing happened. Then he heard soft music, and he peeped over the

top of the rock. Yes, there were the lights coming in from the sea, dancing up and down on the water. He crept down to the water's edge. The lights came closer, and he saw two canoes and people holding torches. These were the dancing lights, then. Kahukura was disappointed. Had he come all this way just to see men fishing at night?

Kahukura had seen fish heads lying on the beach in the late afternoon, but he could not remember any marks of feet on the sand.

"That's funny," he thought. "The fishers must have come from here."

He looked up again. The canoes were much closer, and the fish were jumping out of the water and falling back with a splash. He had never seen so many fish at one time. Then he noticed something else. There was a half circle lying stretching from one canoe to the other, as if a rope were lying on top of the water. It was getting smaller and smaller. The water seemed as if it were boiling and the fish were jumping and splashing everywhere. No sound came from the fishers.

They paddled the canoes right up to the beach. Then they jumped out and began to pull on two long ropes. As they did so the half circle on the water became smaller. One of the men, who seemed to be the chief, said in a musical voice, "Pull the net up quickly."

"I wonder what a 'net' can be?" Kahukura thought as he stood behind a flax bush, hidden in the darkness.

He soon found out. As the fishers tugged at the ropes they had been pulling a net up on to the beach. Then Kahukura knew what it was for! The fish were flapping helplessly on the sand. The men dropped the net and picked up the fish. Then they began to tie them on flax strings. Kahukura left the bush he had been hiding behind and began to help. Suddenly he stepped on a fish and slipped. As he fell he put out a hand to steady himself and touched one of the fishers on the arm. It was cold and wet like a fish, and Kahukura knew that these were not men but sea fairies.

"What shall I do?" he thought. "I know! When the sun comes up they will have to go back to the sea or they will be burnt up. If I can keep them here long enough they will hurry away so quickly that they will have to leave the net behind."

He went on picking up the fish but he did not tie a knot at the end of the string. As soon as he had three or four fish on the line they fell off. When the sea fairies had put their fish in the canoes they came to help Kahukura, thinking he was one of themselves.

"Look out," Kahukura shouted. "The sun is coming up."

They turned and looked out to sea. Sure enough the sun was beginning to peep over the edge of the sea. They rushed to their canoes, but as they were getting in the sun bounded up from the sea, and the fairies and their canoes vanished. All that was left was the fishing net. Kahukura wrapped it up carefully, put it on his back, and began the long walk to his home.

He was very tired when he reached the village. His people were glad to see him again.

"Where have you been?" they asked. "What are you carrying on your back?"

"Come down to the beach and I will show you how we can catch all the fish we need. This is a fishing net. I took it from the sea fairies. It is made of dried flax leaves knotted together. These floats stop it from sinking. The stones at the bottom hold it down so that the fish will swim into it. When we pull it in to the beach it will be full of fish. In a few days we will have enough fish to last us all winter."

When they tried it out, the net worked just as Kahukura said it would, and soon the women were cooking fish for everyone.

The oldest man in the village said to his friends, "The chief was waiting for something to come from the sea, wasn't he? Remember how he used to go down to the beach every day? It wouldn't come to him, so he went and got it from the sea fairies, all

by himself. Now that we know how a fishing net is made, our children must hand this knowledge to their children and their children's children for ever and ever."

THE ADVENTURES OF IHENGA

We have been reading stories of the fairies of New Zealand. Ihenga was a Maori chief who came to Rotorua long ago, before anyone else lived there and was nearly caught by the fairy goblins of Mount Ngongotaha. Ihenga crossed the lake in his canoe and landed at the place that was later called Ngongotaha.

He heard someone singing in the forest, and climbed the mountain to find out who was there. Out of the corner of his eye he could see people or animals (he was not sure which) looking at him through the leaves. Twigs snapped under his feet, but the strange people of the bush made no sound as they fluttered like birds through the branches. They were so quiet that Ihenga was frightened and wondered if they were dangerous, but he wanted to explore the mountain, so he went on until he came to the top.

To his surprise he found a village with a tall fence round it. Close by there was a tree that was on fire. By this time it was beginning to grow dark. Ihenga could feel that the strange forest people were drawing closer. A branch of the tree burnt through and crashed on to the ground. Ihenga picked it up, and turned round just as the fairies made a rush at him. He swung the burning branch round in circles and threw it into some dry teatree. It caught on fire at once and the fairies drew back, covering their eyes against the bright light. Ihenga ran between them as fast as he could. He didn't stop until he reached his canoe.

The next week he went round the lake, looking for a place to build a house and settle down. In the end he came back to where he had first landed. There were birds in the forest, eels in the stream, and ducks and fish in the lake, so he would always have enough to eat. It was here that he settled and built a home for himself.

As time went by he made a garden to grow vegetables, and was very happy. He was kept busy all day long. He even made friends with the fairy people of the mountain, who sometimes came down to the edge of the bush to talk to him. They often sang their sad songs to him and asked him to come and live with them in their village on the top of the mountain.

"You must be lonely, living here all by yourself," they said. "You would be much more comfortable with us. We would sing you to sleep every night."

"No thank you!" Ihenga said. "I want much brighter music than your sad songs."

"Well, come up just for one day, please. We would like you to see our village even if you don't make your home there."

Ihenga thought about it for a while. At last he said, "All right. I'll come up tomorrow."

But somehow he didn't feel happy at the thought of going into the fairy village. There was something strange about these goblin people. Then he said to himself that he was being silly. There was nothing to be afraid of. After all, he was a man and they were not likely to do anything to hurt him.

So next morning he set off and soon reached the top of the mountain. He went into the village. He peeped inside the houses, and looked at the carvings on the doors and windows and the food stores while the fairy people stood round and talked to him.

Presently he felt thirsty. A young woman came up to him and gave him a calabash of water to drink —but the water was enchanted. He wanted to lie down and never get up again, but he knew that if he did, he would never be able to go back to his own home. He would have to stay in the fairy village for ever.

He turned round and raced through the gate and down the mountain path, with the fairies all chasing after him. The young woman who had given him a drink from her calabash had nearly reached him and was stretching out her hands to hold him back until her friends caught up with him. Without stopping, Ihenga felt in the pocket of his belt and pulled out a small piece of cooked food, and some red ochre. He knew that fairies and goblins were afraid of cooked food and red ochre, so he rubbed them over himself.

The young woman fell back. Ihenga crashed through the bushes and did not stop until he reached his own house. He knew that the fairies would not come near him now, but it had been a narrow escape. After his adventure he never went out without cooked food and red ochre in his pocket.

It is said that because of what happened that day the mountain was called Ngongotaha. "Ngongo" is the Maori word for mouthpiece; "taha" is the word for calabash; and so the name Ngongotaha was given because Ihenga drank enchanted water from the mouthpiece of the fairy calabash.

But there are others who say that the name was really given because the mountain looks like a calabash lying on its side.

What do you think?

TAWHAKI'S LONG CLIMB

Tawhaki's wife was very unhappy. She had gone away to her home in the sky, taking her baby girl with her. The trouble was that Tawhaki had said something that hurt her.

"I can't live with you any more, Tawhaki," she cried. "You will have to live by yourself again and learn not to say things that hurt other people."

She caught the baby up in her arms and floated up into the sky.

"I'm coming too," Tawhaki shouted. "I know you are going up to the sky land. You can't escape me like this."

He went to see his brother Karihi. "Hapai has left me," he said. "She was hurt by something I said to her this morning but I still love her. I can't live without her, so I'm going up to the sky too, where I can be with her for ever."

"How are you going to get up to the sky?" Karihi said. "You talk as if it was as easy as walking down to the beach."

"I know a way. It may be dangerous, but I don't care. I've got to get back to Hapai and my little daughter."

"Then I'll come too," Karihi said. "Come on, brother. If we've got to go we might as well start at once."

They went on for a long way, over mountains and across rivers and swamps until they came to a place where roots of a vine hung down like ropes from the sky.

"This is the place where we can climb up to the sky," Tawhaki said.

"Not up the roots of this vine?" Karihi asked in alarm.

"Yes, right up to the top of the vine. Our grandmother lives here. She holds the end of the roots in her hand. She is blind, you know. It won't be easy, and if we're not careful she will try to stop us."

They crept up to her quietly and watched her for a while. There were ten kumaras in front of her, and the old woman was counting them.

"One, two, three, four, five, six, seven, eight, nine, ten," she said, touching them with her fingers.

She began again. "One, two, three, four, five, six seven, eight, nine"—but before she reached "ten" Tawhaki quietly took one of the kumaras away.

"That's funny," the old woman said.

She began again. "One, two, three, four, five, six, seven, eight." This time it was Karihi who picked up a kumara.

She put out her hand again and said very slowly, "One, two, three, four, five, six, seven . . . "

Then she knew that someone was there, taking her kumaras away. She jumped up, let the vine roots

go, and swung a big stick round her head. The two brothers lay flat on the ground as the stick whirred round.

Grandmother heard them laughing and she knew who they were.

"Is that you, Tawhaki and Karihi?" she cried. "You naughty boys. What do you want with your old grandmother?"

"I'm looking for my wife. She has taken our baby up to the sky land," said Tawhaki.

"And how do you think you'll be able to reach her?"

"We want to climb up the roots of the vine that are hanging down here."

"Oh, my poor boy, no one has ever managed to get to the top. Every one who has tried has fallen off before they were half way up. It's not like a ladder, you know."

"We'll be very careful, grandmother."

"Yes, you'll need to be careful. There's just one think you must remember. Always look up. What ever you do, never look down, or you'll get giddy and you'll fall off."

Karihi had not taken any notice of what his grandmother said. While she was talking he caught hold of the roots and began to climb up them.

"Come back," his grandmother called. "You'll fall off if you don't listen to what I say."

"I'm all right," Karihi shouted. "I know what to do."

He kept on climbing and got higher and higher. He could see his grandmother and his brother a long way off. They looked as small as flies crawling on the ground. Karihi began to feel giddy. Then the wind began to blow. The vine roots swung from side to side. Karihi felt sick.

"Don't look down! Look up!" Tawhaki shouted, but Karihi could not hear him. His fingers opened and he slipped down the root. He managed to catch hold of it again, but he was not strong enough to hold fast. Sliding and falling, he reached the ground.

"I've had enough! No one could climb up to the sky on that," he said, pointing at the vine. "I'm going home. He said goodbye to his grandmother and went off.

"I told you what would happen," the old lady said to Tawhaki. "The best thing for you to do is to go home too."

"I said I was going to find my wife, and that's what I'll do even if it kills me. Get out of the way, grandmother."

He rubbed his hands together, choosing the strongest root, and started the long climb. He went slowly, resting from time to time so that he wouldn't get tired. His grandmother's words rang in his head —"Look up! Don't look down." He kept his eyes on the thin thread of the vine where it seemed to vanish in the clouds.

He could just hear his grandmother's voice now —"Hold fast, Tawhaki, hold fast. Let your hands hold fast."

Then her voice died away and he was only half way between earth and sky. The wind tried to blow him away, but he held on fast. It was cold in the thin air, but he kept himself warm by keeping on moving. He climbed through cloud after cloud until at last he came to the blue sky. The earth was a long way off, but he had not come to the end of his long climb.

The sun was setting when he reached the top of the vine, and he came to another land where the same sun was shining brightly. Tawhaki lay on his back on the soft green grass.

"Somewhere in this land I shall find my wife,"

he thought. "I have taken the first step on the long journey that will bring my wife and my little girl back to me again. Now I must rest and sleep for a little while. I'm sure I'll find them before long."

And, after many more adventures, Tawhaki did find his wife and baby girl, and lived happily with them in the sky land.

The Battle Of The Birds

ILLUSTRATIONS:
The Battle of the Birds, JOE BLEAKLEY and JULIA MORISON. *How the Kumara was Brought to New Zealand,* JOHN VINCENT. *What Parrot Stole From Parakeet,* MARK TUCKER. *The Ant and the Cicada,* PAUL CRAIG. *The Mosquito and the Sandfly,* PRU MEXTED. *The Kauri and the Whale,* CHRISTINE BROWN. *The Mussel and the Pipi,* MERLE RENNER.

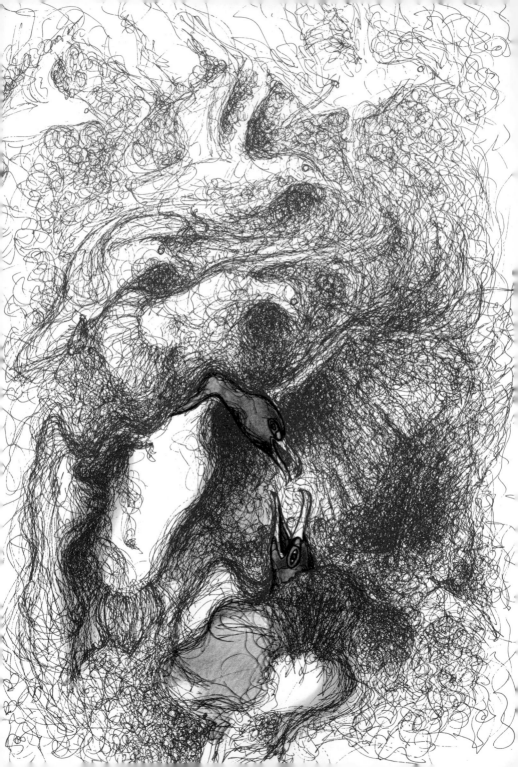

THE BATTLE OF THE BIRDS

River Shag and Sea Shag were cousins. One day River Shag left his home by a stream near the big swamp and flew down the river to see his cousin.

"Hullo!" said the Sea Shag. "What are you doing here?"

"It's a long time since I saw you last," his cousin said. "I wondered how you were getting on."

"That's very kind of you," said Sea Shag. "I'm very well. And how are you?"

"I'm well too, cousin, but I'm hungry after my long trip down the river."

"Then come here and I'll give you something to eat."

Sea Shag spread his wings and flapped over the waves. Then he closed them and dropped like a stone into the water. He came up with a fish in his beak and gave it to his cousin. River Shag swallowed the fish. He closed his eyes and shook his head.

"Oh, oh," he whispered. "I liked it, but it hurt."

"Never mind," his cousin said. "You'll soon get used to it. It's the scales of the fish that hurt you. All fish have scales."

"I can show you lots of fish that have no scales. Come with me tomorrow and you'll see for yourself."

The next day the two birds flew to the swamp and perched on the branch of a tree close to the water.

"Watch!" said River Shag.

He dived into the water and came up with a big fat eel in his beak. Sea Shag swallowed it and laughed.

"Oh, lovely, lovely!" he cried. "No scales! Let me stay here and live with you. I'll help you eat some of these funny fish."

Then River Shag was sorry that he had asked his cousin to come to the swamp.

"Go away!" he shouted. "I don't want anyone to help me eat my lovely eels."

Sea Shag flew away and spread the news of the wonderful fish without scales that could be caught in his cousin's swamp. "But he wouldn't let me stay with him. Let's go up there now and frighten him away," he said to his friends.

All the sea birds agreed with him. They came together from every part of the beach and flew up the river towards River Shag's swamp.

On the morning of the battle River Shag called all the land birds together.

"My cousin the Sea Shag is coming here with a lot of other birds to fight us," he told them. "We must be ready for them, or they will drive us all away. Who'll be the scout?"

"I'll be the scout," said Cuckoo. "With my sharp eyes I'll see when they are coming."

Soon Cuckoo saw many birds flying towards them from the sea.

"*Koo-oo-ee!*" he cried.

Then they heard the battle cry of Seagull, loud and clear.

"Who'll give our battle cry?" asked River Shag.

"I," said Parrot. "I'll give a scream that will frighten the sea birds."

"Who'll do the battle dance?" asked River Shag.

"I," said Fantail. "With my fluttering tail, I'll do the battle dance."

When the dance was ended River Shag looked at his soldiers.

"Who'll begin the fight?" he asked.

"I'll begin the fight," shouted Morepork. "With my beak and claws I'll begin the fight."

He flew up from his perch on the branch of a tree and headed for the sea birds. All the land birds were close behind him, flying and climbing and crawling and hopping and fluttering and diving and zooming and crashing down on the sea birds, hissing and shouting and singing and quacking and snapping and screaming and screeching and squeaking and squawking.

Oh what a fight it was! It lasted from early in the morning until late in the afternoon. Beaks and claws were red with blood, and the swamp soon grew white with fallen feathers.

At first the sea birds seemed to be winning. They drove the land birds in front of them like rain drops in a storm. But there were more land birds than sea birds. Slowly they began to win the battle and as night was falling they drove them back. The sea birds turned tail and flew home.

"*Quack, quack, quack,*" laughed Duck as the sea-gulls flew away.

Now there is peace. Sometimes, in stormy weather, the land birds even let the seagulls come to their home to look for worms and insects, because there is enough food for all the birds that belong to the great god Tane.

III

HOW THE KUMARA WAS BROUGHT TO
NEW ZEALAND

Tere was a very naughty little boy. He was spoiled by his father, whose name was Pou, and his mother. They gave Tere everything he asked for because he cried when he couldn't get his own way.

While Tere was still young, long before he had learned to talk, he began to poke out his tongue. Lots of babies do that, of course, but the strange thing was that he never poked it out to the south or the east or the west, but always to the north.

"I wonder why he does it," Pou said to his wife.

"He must be hungry," she said. "Perhaps he wants some kind of food that is found only in the north."

"I don't know what it can be," said Father Pou. "It must be a long, long way off, but what ever it is, I'll go and look for it."

He dragged his canoe down the beach and pushed it into the water. He paddled over the waves. Presently the wind began to blow. He put his paddle in the bottom of the canoe and pulled up the sail. Day after day and night after night the canoe sailed on, until at last it came to a land that Pou had never seen before.

He jumped out of the canoe and pulled it up on to the beach. He soon made friends with the people who came to meet him.

"You must be hungry after your long voyage,"

they said. "Come and eat with us."

They sat down on the grass while girls brought baskets full of meat and hot vegetables. Pou pointed to one of the vegetables.

"What is this?" he asked. "I have never seen a vegetable like that before."

They looked at him in surprise.

"Do you like it?" they asked. "It is called kumara. It is a root vegetable."

Pou was excited. "This must be what Tere wants!" he said, and he told his new friends how his son kept on poking out his tongue as if he knew where to find what he wanted.

They laughed and clapped their hands.

"If that is all you want," they said, "you can take some seed kumaras back with you in your canoe. You will have to plant them carefully and keep them well watered. Then you'll have as many kumaras as you want."

Pou was very happy. He lay awake for a long time that night listening to the wind in the trees and the waves roaring up the beach. He thought how pleased Tere would be when he saw the kumaras his father had come such a long way to find.

But when Pou went down to the beach next morning, his canoe had gone. It had been taken away by the wind and the waves!

"Whatever shall I do?" Pou asked his friends. "My canoe has gone!"

"Never mind, Pou," the chief said. "I will help you to get back to your home. I'll lend you my giant bird. He is called the Great Bird of Rua."

"I've heard of the Great Bird of Rua," Pou whispered, "but how can he help me?"

The chief smiled. "The bird will carry you across the sea to your own land," he said. "He is a very large bird. When you climb on to his back you must hold on tight and he will carry you home."

"There is only one thing to be careful about. When you are halfway home you will pass an island. It is very dangerous, because it is the home of the ogre Tama. If he catches you he will kill you."

"What must I do?" Pou asked.

"You must wait until the sun is setting. It will shine right into Tama's eyes and he won't see you. You'll be able to fly past him before he can catch you. When you get home please remember to send the bird back to me. If you don't send him at once, Tama is sure to catch him."

Early the next morning the chief gave Pou two baskets full of kumaras, and helped him climb on to the back of the Great Bird of Rua.

"Are you ready?" he called.

"Quite ready," shouted Pou.

The Great Bird ran along the beach. He flapped his big wings and lifted Pou and the baskets. Pou looked down and saw his friend the chief waving to him. He waved back until he could see him no longer.

The bird flew on. Sometimes Pou could see clouds
below him, and sometimes he saw the blue sea and
the white caps of the waves. Then, as the sun began
to sink, he saw the island where Tama the ogre
lived. He tugged at the bird's head and he flew

more slowly until the edge of the sun touched the sea.

"Come on!" he shouted and the bird flew quickly past the island. Tama heard the sound of its wings and rushed out, but he could not see because the sun was in his eyes.

Pou was tired. He wanted to get home quickly and give some of his kumaras to Tere.

He forgot that his friend the chief had told him to be sure to let the Great Bird go home as soon as he reached his own country.

"I expect you're tired too," he said to the bird. "You can have a good feed and a night's sleep and then tomorrow I'll let you go home."

So while the Great Bird was resting, Pou told his friends where he had been and what he had done. He cooked three of the kumaras so everyone could taste them. Tere was pleased too. He wanted more, but his father said, "No. You must wait. I have to plant them now. We must wait a long time before you can have another taste."

Ever since the Maoris of New Zealand have grown kumaras from the seeds that Pou brought with him on the back of the Great Bird of Rua.

But, for the friendly chief who had given the kumaras to Pou, the days passed slowly and sadly. He was waiting for his bird to come back to him, but Pou had kept him too long. Tama caught him as he tried to fly past his island and ate him up.

WHAT PARROT STOLE FROM PARAKEET

Once upon a time Parakeet had a beautiful red breast. Dressed in his green coat and shiny red shirt he was indeed a good-looking bird. Poor old Parrot's feathers looked quite dusty and brown.

"You silly bird," he said. "You should try to hide that red breast of yours."

"Why should I hide my feathers?" Parakeet asked. "I'm sure that everyone likes my feathers.

Red, red as the blood of Kai-tangata,
Red, red as the sky at sunset,
Red, red as the flowers of the Christmas tree,
Oh my beautiful red feathers," he sang.

"Oh my dear little cousin," Parrot said, "You don't know how silly you are. When Tane gave me my brown feathers he gave me the very best present he had. Brown is the colour of Mother Earth under the green grass. The insects cannot see me until I snap them up in my beak. Brown is the colour that Tane loves."

"But Tane covered Mother Earth with green," Parakeet said, coming closer to Parrot, "and red is the colour of the coat he put on Father Sky to make him beautiful too. Surely Tane loves red and green best of all?"

"No, Parakeet. This may make you sad, but he has not really loved you at all, or he would never have given you those funny-looking feathers."

Parakeet ruffled his feathers and tried to hide his shiny red shirt by covering it with his wings.

"What can I do?" he asked sadly. "Tane gave them to me. I shall have to keep them all my life unless I can give them to another bird who is willing to give me his feathers."

"There is only one way," Parrot said, thumping Parakeet on the back with his claw. "No one else would do this for you, cousin, but I feel sorry for you. Because I love you so much I will take your red feathers and hide them under my wings where no one can see them."

Parakeet pulled out his red feathers and gave them to Parrot who quickly tucked them under his

wings. Then he gave some of his brown feathers to Parakeet who used them to cover his bare breast.

"Look at me! Look at me!" squawked Parrot. He spread his beautiful wings so that everyone could see the red feathers that Parakeet had given him and sailed over the tree tops.

When Parakeet saw how beautiful Parrot had become, he knew that his cousin had stolen the best thing that his Father Tane had ever given him. He cried and cried while Parrot zoomed over the tree-tops and proudly called to the other birds of the forest to come and see how beautiful he had become.

Now Parakeet's coat is green, but Parrot has bright red feathers as well as brown for all the world to see.

But the little Parakeet is not as sad as we might think.

"I know I lost my red feathers because I listened to Parrot's honeyed words," he says. "It's a good job he didn't try to take the green ones away. That's the colour that Tane loves best of all. You don't see him using red very often—only a little bit in the sky and only at night and morning, and in a few flowers that soon fall to the ground.

"Green is best, or else he wouldn't have used it for grass and trees when he wanted to make Mother Earth look so beautiful."

THE ANT AND THE CICADA

Have you ever heard the cicadas singing in the New Zealand forest in summer? The sun shines through the leaves. The warm wind makes them dance in the sunshine, and winter seems far away.

This is the song that Cicada sings:

Winter is past and summer is here.
Let us sing our song on the warm bark
    of the trees and be glad,
For cold and darkness have gone away for
    ever.

The ants have a song too, but hardly anyone has ever heard it because of the noise the cicadas make.

Here is the song of the Ant:

> Winter is coming.
> We need food to keep us alive
> In the cold winter days.
> Let us work now
> So we can live through the winter.

All the time Ant is singing he keeps on working, picking up tiny pieces of food and carrying them to his food store under the ground.

The long summer days begin to grow short. The leaves that danced in the sunshine shiver in the cold, winter wind. The rain pours down and the brown leaves flutter to the ground.

Then Cicada, who was warm and happy and did nothing but sing through the summer days, grows thin and cold. He crawls into cracks in the bark of the trees and shivers in the wind.

But Ant is still happy, for he is warm and well fed in his comfortable nest under the trees, waiting until summer comes once more and it is time to get ready for another winter.

THE MOSQUITO AND THE SANDFLY

One day Mosquito and Sandfly met beside a dark pool in the forest.

"Who can we fight today?" asked Namu the Sandfly.

"I know," said Mosquito. "Let's have a fight with Man. He is big and strong but if we attack him together we'll soon make him sorry."

Sandfly danced up and down excitedly.

"Good!" he said. "Let's go at once. Let's taste the blood of Man!"

"Steady!" said Mosquito. "You are in too much of a hurry. If we attack him now he will see us coming and he will kill us before we can get close to him. Wait until night comes. Man cannot see at night. Then will be the time to attack him."

"I shall not wait," Namu said. "My people will make their attack in the light of the sun. Many of them will be killed, of course, but we shall defeat him."

He called his brothers, and together they flew like a black cloud over the trees to fight against Man.

The afternoon passed slowly by while Mosquito waited by the pool for Sandfly and his brothers to come back. As the sun was sinking he looked up and saw Sandfly flying towards him all alone.

"Where are your brothers?" he asked.

"Gone," said Sandfly sadly. "All gone."

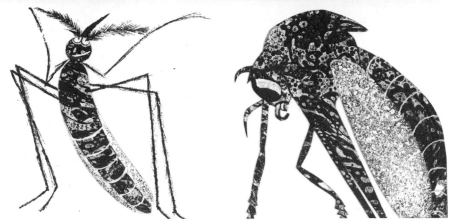

"Why, what happened? Didn't you win the battle?"

Sandfly bowed his head and sang the song of defeat.

"We tasted blood," he said when the song was ended. "Man could not stop us. But man is very strong. Slap! went his big hand and many of my brothers were killed. Slap! went his hand again and more of my brothers were killed. Now all my brothers are dead, and I am the only one left."

"You were silly to begin the battle by day," Mosquito said. "I told you so, but you wouldn't listen."

"I shall never give in," said Sandfly proudly. "I shall attack him again and again."

"You must do as you please," Mosquito said, "but remember, you have been defeated because you attacked by day. My way is best. Now it is dark, and I'm on my way."

He winged his way over the trees by the light of the stars, and all the Mosquitoes followed him.

Man did not know they were coming until suddenly he heard the whine of many wings in his house. The sound came closer. Then the whining stopped.

"Oh dear," said Man. He sat up in the darkness.

"That must be Mosquito and all his family. They have settled on me to drink my blood. I'll kill them just as I killed Sandfly and his brothers this afternoon."

He slapped his arm, but Mosquito was not there. Now the whine of many wings was close to his ear. He slapped himself until his head rang, but by this time Mosquito was standing on his leg drinking his blood.

He sat up and slapped but Mosquito was gone and three of his brothers were settling on his shoulder.

All through the night Man kept on fighting the Mosquito people. Soon he was covered in blood. When morning came only two Mosquitoes had been killed by his slapping hand. The rest of them flew away before the sun rose.

Sandfly heard the Mosquito people long before he could see them. They were singing the song of victory. He was glad to know that his friends had at last won the battle with Man.

They still fight against Man, Sandfly by day and Mosquito by night—but Man is more afraid of Mosquitoes than he is of Sandflies.

THE KAURI AND THE WHALE

The Whale is the biggest animal that lives in the sea, and the Kauri tree is the tallest thing that grows on land.

The giant tree stands straight and strong, waving its great branches in the wind. If you look at the trunk of the Kauri you will see that it is smooth and grey, and you can find sticky gum on it in some places. Once upon a time men used to look for this gum in the branches of the tree, and to dig for it in the ground where Kauri trees once grew. It is called Kauri gum.

The giant of the sea and the giant of the forest became friends. Whale swam close to the cliff where Kauri was growing.

"Come with me," he called. "If you stay here, men will cut you down to make a canoe. It is not safe for you to stay there."

Kauri shook his leafy arms.

"Who am I to care for funny little men?" he said proudly. "They can't hurt me."

"You don't really know much about them," Whale said. "They may be small, but they have sharp adzes that can eat into you, and fire that can burn you. Come with me before it is too late."

"No, no, my dear friend," Kauri said. "If you came to live with me on the land you would be helpless. You would not be able to move about as you do in the sea. And if I were to go with you I would be helpless when the storms tossed me about. My leaves would drop off and I would sink to the bottom of the sea and drown. I would no longer see the bright sun or feel the rain on my leaves. No longer would I be able to stand up and fight the wind while my roots hold me close to Mother Earth."

Whale thought for a while. At last he said, "Yes, you are quite right. I would drown as quickly on land as you would in water. But you are my friend, and I want to help you. Let us change our skins so that we will always remember each other."

He took off his smooth grey skin and gave it to Kauri. Then Kauri gave him his bark. The two friends wrapped each other's skins round themselves.

"Thank you, thank you," they said.

Whale swam away feeling proud of his new skin. Kauri stayed on the edge of the cliff. He too was proud of the smooth grey skin wrapped round his trunk.

Today the Kauri trees that grow in the north of New Zealand still have plenty of gum, just as the Whale has plenty of oil in his big body. And both still proudly wear their smooth grey skins.

THE MUSSEL AND THE PIPI

Kuku the mussel and Pipi the cockle and their families had been fighting one another on the beach. The cockles had lost and were digging deep into the sand to get away from the mussels. Kuku said to his friends, "Don't let them get away. Hurry, or we'll lose them."

The mussels climbed over the seaweed as quickly as they could and tried to dig the cockles up with their tongues, but soon they were covered with sand, and had to go back to the rocks at the end of the beach to wash it out.

That is why mussels still make their homes among the rocks, while the cockles dig deep into the sand on the beaches.

Te Pu the whale and Taka the shark had been watching Kuku and Pipi fighting. They thought it was all very funny.

"What's the matter with the little people?" asked Te Pu.

"They each want all the beach for themselves," Taka said.

"Is that all?" laughed Te Pu. "I'd like to give them something better than that to fight about. Our children are hungry. Let's go up on to the beach and have a good feed of mussels and cockles. Then they will really have something to fight for."

Taka shook his head. "It wouldn't do any good,"

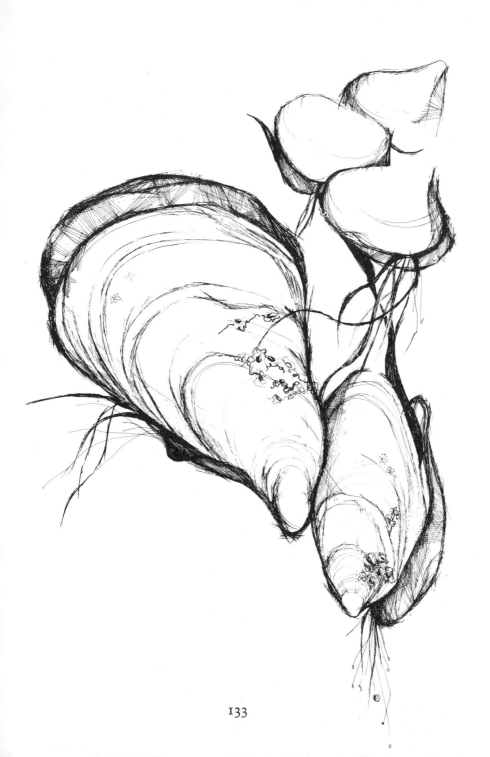

he said. "They would just go into the sand and hide among the rocks where we couldn't reach them."

"You can do what you like," said Te Pu, "but I'm going with my children to have a feed of mussels and cockles."

He swam ashore with all his children. It was easy sliding over the wet seaweed, but crawling over the sand and climbing over the rocks was much harder.

The mussels crawled up the rocks so quickly that the whale children could not catch them. They hurt themselves on the sharp edges of the rocks and rolled down on to the beach again.

"Go for the cockles," Te Pu shouted. "You won't hurt yourselves in the sand."

The cockles heard him and scrambled out of the way.

"Dig quickly," Pipi cried. "The whales are coming. Go for your lives!"

So the cockles hid themselves in the sand. When the whales tried to pull them out, their blow holes became filled with sand and they were soon dead.

"Whales sometimes swim too close to the beach, and are left there when the tide goes out," Maori mothers tell their little children. "I expect they were silly enough to try to get another feed of cockles."

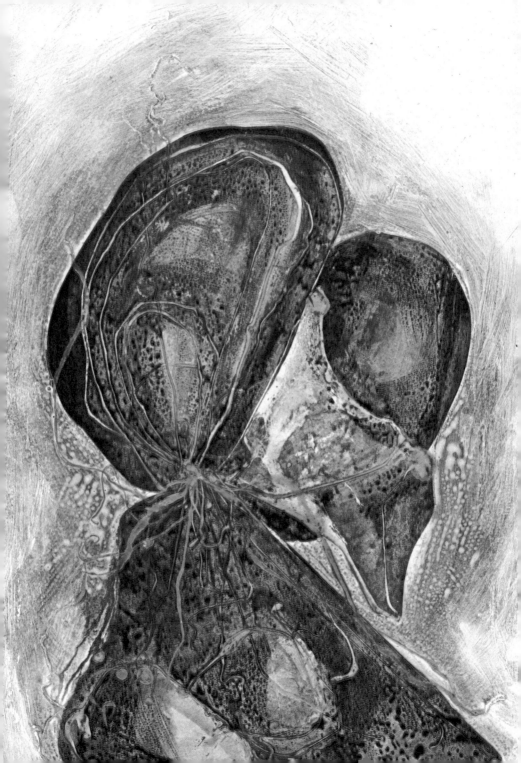

OTHER REED BOOKS

MAORI FAIRY TALES
A. W. Reed
The rich story of Maori legend written for very young children, with large type and short, easy-to-read sentences. Delightfully illustrated in two-colour line by Ray Labone.
$8\frac{1}{2}$ x $5\frac{1}{2}$ in, 112 pages, 2-colour illustrations on every page, cased.

MAORI LEGENDS
A. W. Reed
Maori legends presented in a charming way – stories of Maori creation, the underworld, the gods, Kupe and Maui, etc. Imaginative illustrations by Roger Hart.
$9\frac{3}{4}$ x $7\frac{1}{4}$ in, 48 pages, casebound, full colour laminated jacket.

LET'S LOOK AT NEW ZEALAND
A. W. Reed
A magnificent pictorial book that tells young people (and older ones too) all about New Zealand – from her mountains, rivers, lakes, plants, and birds to local government, defence, science, and how money is earned and spent.
11 x $8\frac{1}{2}$ in, 64 pages, illustrated in full colour throughout, stapled paper covers.

WONDER TALES OF MAORILAND
A. W. Reed
A frequently reprinted selection of Maori Legends retold by Popo, the village storyteller, to his two young companions, Rata and Hine. Illustrated by A. S. Paterson.
$9\frac{1}{2}$ x $7\frac{1}{4}$ in, 144 pages, 76 line drawings, casebound.